D0298010

This book belongs to

PRUSS

....

RUSLAN................

This is a Parragon book
This edition first published 2005

Parragon Publishing
Queen Street House
4 Queen Street
Bath, BA1 1HE

Copyright © 2005 Disney Enterprises, Inc.
Based on the "Winnie the Pooh" works,
by A. A. Milne and E. H. Shepard

All rights reserved. No part of this publication may be reproduced,
stored in a retrieval system, or transmitted by any other means,
electronic, mechanical, photocopying, recording, or otherwise,
without the prior permission of the copyright holder.

ISBN 1-40546-051-2

Printed in China

Disney
Winnie the Pooh
Storytime Treasury

Contents

p

Rainy Day

It was a fine, sunny afternoon, and the sun was shining brightly, as it is supposed to do on sunny afternoons. Pooh and Piglet went to visit Rabbit.

'Good day,' said Pooh as he raised his paw to cover his eyes from the glare of the sun.

'Good day,' said Piglet, lowering his ears to shade his eyes.

'It's not a good day for me,' grumbled Rabbit. 'The ground is so dry nothing will grow!'

Rabbit looked up at the sky. 'Those clouds in the distance… They had better burst into rain before my plants wilt completely,' he said.

'You're right, Rabbit,' Piglet said. 'Your vegetables do need rain, but I like sunny days better than rainy ones,' he sighed.

'*Boing!*'

The friends turned round.
They knew this sound very well
– and they knew who was making
it! Tigger!

'Piglet, you look worried,' Tigger said
as he landed.

Piglet blinked. 'Rabbit said the clouds are going to
burst and that it's going to storm! It's
so loud when it storms!'

Tigger inspected the
horizon. 'Storm?
I see Pooh, I see
Rabbit, I see
Piglet... but
I don't see any
clouds at all!'

'Really?' Piglet asked, and looked around himself just to be sure.

'Yes, really!' Tigger said, and bounced around, knocking Pooh and Piglet onto their backs.

This is how Piglet and Pooh came to be lying on their backs, looking at the sky.

And from this angle, they were finally able to see some clouds coming into view.

'As usual, there are those who can lie around whilst others work!' growled Rabbit. He grabbed his watering can and went to get some water. 'If only it would rain, for heaven's sake.'

As soon as Rabbit left, a group of tiny white clouds passed above our friends. 'Look carefully, Piglet,' said Pooh. 'Here comes a big sheep right above us!'

'It looks more like a pig to me. Oh, Pooh, look! There is a big pillow running after it!'

Pooh didn't answer. He was counting. The clouds had started to look like honey pots, and they were becoming bigger and rounder!

'I would need another cupboard if I had to store all this honey,' Pooh thought to himself.

'Oh! Oh! Oh!' Tigger cried. 'Here comes a cloud that looks just like Eeyore!'

A grey cloud had appeared and the sunlight made it shimmer nicely.

'But I never saw Eeyore smile like that!' joked Tigger with a hearty laugh.

Suddenly, the shuffle of Eeyore's weary feet could be heard. 'If I were you,' Eeyore sighed, gloomily, 'I wouldn't laugh. Bad weather is coming again.'

'But Tigger said the clouds wouldn't bring rain,' Piglet protested.

Everyone could see that Piglet was afraid.

'The wind that blew these clouds is getting stronger and stronger! We should take cover,' insisted Eeyore.

There was a deep rumble.

'Well,' Pooh observed, 'there's a rumbly in my tummy. It must be time for a snack. You are all invited to my house!'

There was another rumble.

'That was the storm this time,' Eeyore said.

'Well, it looks as if I'm going to get wet again.'

Eeyore had barely finished speaking when it started to rain. It not only started, but it continued raining, gently at first, then heavier.

'Could we go to my house instead?' asked Piglet, whose teeth were chattering. 'It's much closer!'

Pooh, Rabbit and Eeyore followed Piglet home. When they walked through the door, Piglet was nowhere to be found!

Suddenly, lightning struck, lighting the room.
There was Piglet, under his bed!

'What are you doing under the bed, Piglet?' Pooh
asked. 'Are you all right?'

Piglet didn't answer. A rumble of thunder
answered instead.

'It sounds like the rumbly of my
tummy,' Pooh decided. 'Do you
think the sky is hungry?'

RUMBLE!

'I think it's almost as
hungry as I am,' Pooh said
whilst rubbing his round,
empty tummy.

Soon, thanks to the wind, the clouds were
blown further away, and the
storm followed them.

'Oh! Oh! Oh!' shouted Tigger.
'There are puddles outside.
Tiggers love to bounce over
puddles. Let's go!'

'I'm not going outside,'
protested Piglet.

'But the puddles are waiting
to be jumped over by Piglet, too,'
insisted Tigger.

'And my stomach needs me,'
added Pooh. 'It needs some honey!'

'Are you all leaving?' Piglet asked,
and jumped out from under his bed. 'Don't
leave me alone with the thunder!'

When Piglet stepped outside, instead of a frightening, rainy wood, he saw a lovely Hundred-Acre Wood glistening from the freshly fallen raindrops. Frogs croaked happily, ducks quacked merrily and birds sang loudly.

'Look at all the puddles,' Piglet cried as he started to splash around.

'The best part of a storm is the splish-splashing once it's over,' Pooh exclaimed happily.

But Winnie the Pooh was still very hungry and suggested that he and Piglet stop by his house for a bite to eat.

Eeyore was invited, too, but he had to check on his home. 'It's probably been destroyed,' he said, as he moped away.

So Piglet walked Pooh home. And once the friends had had their fill of honey, Pooh walked Piglet home.

That night, a light fog spread through the Hundred-Acre Wood. When the moon rose, its light shone like a halo through the mist.

Owl spread his wings. 'It looks like a fine and sunny day for tomorrow,' he said.

'Really?' Piglet said, looking a little disappointed. 'I was hoping it would rain again.'

Honey Cake

One day, Piglet went to help Kanga and Roo cook a cake for a tea party. All their friends from the Hundred-Acre Wood were expected.

'Good morning!' said Piglet, as he arrived at Kanga's house. 'I hope I am not late!'

'You're right on time, Piglet,' replied Kanga. 'I need to go out for a little while. Here is what you will have to do... '

'Do you hear that, Piglet?' cried Roo. 'We are going to make the cake all by ourselves, like grown-ups!'

'Oh!' whispered Piglet, doubtfully. 'How will we be able to do that?'

'Don't worry, Piglet,' said Kanga. 'I've written instructions on this board.'

Piglet and Roo looked at the board. It listed so many yummy ingredients they could almost smell the cake cooking!

'Just read the recipe,' reassured Kanga. 'Follow the directions from beginning to end without skipping a step.'

Kanga read the recipe aloud. 'First separate the eggs, putting the yolks into one bowl and the whites into another.' Then add sugar, flour and honey to the egg yolks.'

'Beat the whites until they are stiff, and mix with the other ingredients. Pour into a buttered cake tin,' continued Kanga.

'We understand,' interrupted Roo as he hurried his mother towards the door. 'You can go!'

'Are you sure?' asked Kanga.

'Yes!' said Roo.

'Yes,' confirmed Piglet, though less firmly.

'Look, here comes Winnie the Pooh. He can help,' said Kanga. 'See you all later!'

Pooh came in. When he saw honey written on the board, he understood at once what his job was.

Before they started cooking, Roo and Piglet changed into cook's outfits. They put on aprons, just like Kanga did when she cooked. 'First we'll put all the ingredients on the table,' Roo said excitedly.

Pooh watched as Piglet and Roo put the eggs, flour and sugar on the table next to the honey.

'We must crack the eggs and separate the whites from the yolks,' Piglet read.

As he listened to Piglet and Roo reading the recipe, Pooh came up with a little song.

    Egg yolk, egg white

        Golden honey, sugar bright!

           'I have an idea,' said Roo. 'Why

             don't we ask Pooh to measure out

              the honey?'

             Pooh smiled,

               'It is a truly

               wonderful idea!'

Pooh stood on a chair and lifted the pot to pour some honey into a bowl. As he poured, he caught a droplet stuck on the rim with his paw.

'This drop is stuck to the pot,' Pooh said as he licked his paw. 'I wonder if it will happen again.'

To find out, Pooh poured more honey. It did happen again. So Pooh poured again and again and again, letting the honey drip all over his paws.

'Shall we beat the eggs now?' Piglet suggested.

'Yes,' Roo said. 'We must break them first.'
They broke the eggs, but they forgot to
separate them. Piglet took out the
whisk. Then he and little Roo took
turns mixing.

'Are they stiff enough?' Piglet
asked, as he whisked the mixture
with all his might.

Roo and Piglet put the yellow mixture aside
and picked up the flour. As Roo tapped the bottom
of the bag to get the flour out, the whole bag emptied
into the bowl.

'I think there's too much,' said Piglet.

He was right. The white flour spread all over the
table and covered Piglet up to his nose.

'I'd better try again,' decided Roo,
and he tried to sweep all the flour
back into the bag.

Soon there was more flour outside the bag than inside. Pooh didn't notice. He was sound asleep, his belly full of honey.

'It's snowing!' cried Roo as he threw a handful of flour into the air.

'Now it is time to add the honey,' said Piglet. He tried pouring honey into the bowl, but the honey pot was empty.

Piglet and Roo mixed the yellow mixture with the white flour and poured everything into the cake tin. They carefully put the tin into the oven.

Then Kanga returned home. 'Did everything go alright?' she asked.

'Yes,' said Roo. 'But the kitchen isn't very clean.'

'That's all right, darling,' laughed Kanga. Roo and Piglet sat by the clock impatiently waiting for the cake to cook.

At last, Kanga announced that thirty minutes were up, and the cake was done. Eagerly, they watched as she opened the oven door and took out something rather strange.

'Th-that doesn't look like a cake!' stuttered Piglet.

'Hmmm... are you sure you followed the recipe?' asked Kanga.

'I think we forgot to separate the eggs,' realised Roo.

'Let's bake another cake,' said Kanga.

Piglet read the recipe. Roo made sure Piglet didn't skip anything, and Piglet made sure Roo checked correctly.

The only one who made a mistake this time was Kanga! When Roo and Piglet noticed, they both cried out. Kanga had forgotten to put a pinch of salt in the egg whites!

'I'm so lucky you're here!' she exclaimed.

Half an hour later, a delicious smell came from the kitchen and reached Pooh's nose.

Soon all the guests arrived. Everyone admired the golden cake.

'Mummy baked it!' Roo cried.

'But I couldn't have done it without help from these two little cooks,' Kanga said.

And with that, everyone sat down for afternoon tea.

Hunny Cake Recipe

Ingredients: 3 eggs, 80g sugar, 3 dessert spoons of honey, 90g self raising flour, 1 pinch of salt

- Separate the egg yolks from the whites, and place into two separate bowls.
- Add sugar and honey to the yolks, and beat well.
- Mix in spoonfuls of flour.
  - Add a pinch of salt to the egg whites, and whisk until stiff.
  - Gently mix the egg whites into the yolk mixture.
  - Pour into a round buttered cake tin. Cook for 30 minutes at 180°c, 360°f, Gas 4.
  - Remove from oven and cool.
  - Get a grown-up to cut the cake in half, spread with jam and cream and sandwich together. Decorate the top of your cake with icing.

Enjoy with your friends!

Bad Mood

When Rabbit entered his garden one morning, he knew it was the sort of day when his friends would say, 'Rabbit is in a bad mood!'

His carrots had shrunk, the lettuce had wilted, and the turnips had simply forgotten to grow. He knelt down to pull a radish.

'Oh, what a disaster!' he cried as he took a bite. 'It's too hot and spicy!'

He pulled out another one and another one, but they were as hot as the first.

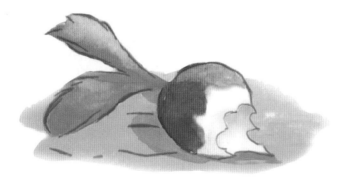

Rabbit turned to his shrunken carrots. Without a word, he pulled them out and threw them as far away as he could.

He looked at his ruined garden, and his bad mood got worse.

'Disaster of disasters!' he said as he jumped up and down.

That's when Rabbit saw Tigger bouncing towards him.

'I'm impressed, Bunny Boy!' Tigger said as Rabbit continued to jump in anger. 'I didn't know you could bounce so well! Will you come and bounce with me?'

'Tigger, I am not in the mood to be merry,' said Rabbit, crossly.

'Really? Well, I'd better go then!' shouted Tigger as he bounced away.

'There! Now I'm on my own,' groaned Rabbit. 'Alone with these wilted lettuce leaves that are only good to be stepped on!' he concluded.

There was not much left of Rabbit's garden when Piglet arrived. He had thought that Rabbit would be happy to see him, but seeing Rabbit's cross face he wasn't so sure.

'Good morning, Rabbit,' Piglet whispered.

'What do you want?' mumbled Rabbit. 'Can't you see I'm in a bad mood?'

'Well, yes Rabbit, I can see that! Oh dear, look at your garden. All the vegetables have been pulled out!' said Piglet.

'I think you'd better go, Piglet,' said Rabbit.
'My bad mood is growing bigger.'

Piglet looked in fright above Rabbit's head. Since
he could see nothing there, he thought he must be
too small to see such a big, bad mood.

Piglet started to tremble. If Rabbit's bad mood
came too close, it might gobble him up!

'G–goodbye, Rabbit!' Piglet stuttered.

Piglet ran straight to Pooh's house to tell him what was going on.

'I *see*,' said Pooh as he thought hard. 'Rabbit doesn't like being in a bad mood.'

Pooh understood so well.

'You say the bad mood is above Rabbit's head, but you can't *see* it?' asked Pooh, as he thought even harder.

'Yes,' confirmed Piglet.

'Dear me,' said Pooh.
'I think the bad mood is
some sort of cloud which
stops Rabbit from being
in a good mood.'

'Maybe it's like a storm inside
his head,' suggested Piglet.
'It looked like there was
lightning in Rabbit's eyes.'

The friends went to Owl's house to ask him what he thought.

'If Rabbit is in a bad mood, and he doesn't like being in a bad mood,' Owl reasoned wisely, 'then the bad mood must be removed from him.'

'With water, to put out the lightning in his eyes?' asked Piglet.

'By blowing away the cloud above his head?' suggested Pooh.

'I think we should try to understand why Rabbit is in a bad mood,' Owl said. 'Then Rabbit's bad mood will go away by itself.'

The three friends headed off to Rabbit's house. Tigger bounced by and joined them.

They found Rabbit in the same spot, leaning on his shovel with an angry face.

'So, I hear you're in a bad mood,' said Owl.

'Can't you see?' grumbled Rabbit.

'We would like to know why you are in a bad mood,' Owl continued.

Rabbit waved his arm at his ruined garden.

'Shrunken carrots, yellow lettuce, hot radishes and not even the smallest little turnip!' he said.

'Could it be that you might have forgotten to water your plants?' Owl reasoned.

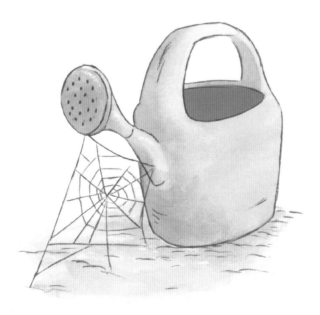

Rabbit clutched his shovel. Piglet was sure he saw streaks of lightning in his eyes.

'Are you suggesting that I did not do my job properly!' cried Rabbit, angrily.

Spreading his wings, Owl turned to his friends. 'This is what I call being in a bad mood,' he said.

'Yes, I am in a bad mood!' cried Rabbit, losing his temper. 'I won't have enough food for winter, and now you're calling me a bad gardener!'

'Of course we know that you haven't made a mistake,' protested Owl. 'You are an excellent gardener!'

'Could it be worms eating Rabbit's seeds?' suggested Piglet.

'Impossible. Gopher ate all the worms last spring,' grumbled Rabbit as Gopher poked his little face out of a hole.

'What if the turnip seeds were still in your cellar and not in the ground at all?' suggested Tigger.

'Hmmm,' muttered Rabbit. Rabbit tried to remember. Now he thought about it, he wasn't so sure that he'd actually planted the seeds at all!

'Maybe it was the bad weather,' added Pooh. 'It rained so much this year. Do you remember we had to cancel a picnic?'

'Oh yes!' recalled Piglet. 'There were so many puddles!'

'And I missed the most beautiful bounce when I got stuck in the mud!' cried Tigger.

'No plants could grow in such conditions,' confirmed Owl.

'This must be what happened!'  exclaimed Rabbit with a smile forming from ear to ear.

'We will help you plant your garden all over again!' declared Pooh. 'Your vegetables will still have plenty of time to grow before winter!'

'If someone asked my opinion about all of this, but I bet no one will,' grumbled Eeyore, 'I would say that a bad mood is like bad weather. It comes and goes, just as the sky can be blue or grey.'

'Aren't Eeyores always grey?' Rabbit asked.

Eeyore nodded, and everyone laughed as they helped a happy Rabbit tend to his garden.

Nap Time

It was a lovely, sunny summer afternoon. All of the friends of the Hundred-Acre Wood were gathered around Tigger, who was explaining how a tigger's springy tail makes them the best bouncers.

Suddenly, Kanga called out to her son. 'Roo! I'm waiting for you, sweetheart!'

Roo pretended he didn't hear.

'Well, Roo,' said Rabbit, 'something tells me it is time for your nap.'

'Are you sure it's nap time?' grumbled a frowning Roo.

'Same time as yesterday, darling,' replied Kanga.

'But I don't feel like taking a nap right now. Couldn't I take one later? I'll sleep extra to catch up, like this.' Roo shut his eyes tightly and made a funny face.

Owl cleared his throat. 'I'm afraid that won't do any good. As my wise old grandmother used to say, if you don't have a proper nap you'll run out of play before the end of the day.'

But Roo ignored Owl and burst out laughing. Tigger had bundled him up and sent him flying like a ball up into the air and back down again.

Kanga held out her arms to catch her little one.

'Time to go now, Roo.'

'Just a minute,' Roo replied. 'I'm playing a bouncing game with Tigger.'

'Remember what Owl said about running out of play!' said Rabbit.

'But I've got heaps left!' Roo grumbled, 'I don't need to nap for more.'

'Anyway, I still don't understand why I should go now,' argued Roo. 'I'm just not tired.'

'We all need lots of rest when we're small,' said Piglet.

Roo pointed up to the sky. 'But nobody else sleeps during the day! The sun doesn't sleep, the sky doesn't sleep, the flowers and the bees don't... '

'Owls sleep during the daytime, Roo,' reasoned Owl.

'Well, at least you get to stay up **all** night to make up for it,' Roo complained.

'You know,' said Pooh, 'I very much like taking afternoon naps, especially after eating a pot of honey.'

'Hey!' added Tigger. 'Just think how much more bouncy you'll feel after a nap!'

With that Tigger threw his paws in the air and twisted his tail in an enormous bounce, landing right on top of poor Eeyore's house.

'Well, I could do with a little nap,' grumbled Eeyore. 'Except now I can't because I don't have a house to nap in.'

Roo looked at Eeyore in surprise. 'Why don't all of you take a nap if you like it so much? I don't want to be the only one asleep while everyone else gets to play.'

'Play?' cried Rabbit. 'We've got work to do!'

'We do?' asked Tigger, surprised.

'Yes we do!' Rabbit laughed. 'Thanks to your silly
bouncing we've got to rebuild poor
Eeyore's house.'

'Thanks for noticing that,'
said Eeyore, gloomily.

'So I won't be missing
out?' asked Roo, with
a little yawn.

'Not a single bounce!'
grinned Tigger, as he
jumped through the
window, right onto
Roo's bed.

Rabbit started collecting lots of sticks straight away.

'Oh bother,' said Pooh as he struggled with two especially awkward ones. 'This is going to be tricky.'

'There's so much to do I don't know where to start!' Piglet cried, following behind.

'Have a good nap!' all of Roo's friends exclaimed, waving goodbye as they set to work.

Once Tigger had sprung back out of the window, Kanga put Roo into bed. 'Sweet dreams, darling!' she whispered.

'We'll play lots of games when I wake up, won't we, Mama?' said Roo, as his head sank into the soft pillow.

'Oh yes,' nodded Kanga as she closed the door, 'Lots and lots of games.'

As soon as he heard the door shut, Roo sat up.

'I'm still not ready to fall asleep,' he said.

Roo climbed out of bed and picked up his toys.

'It's time for you all to take a nap while I do some work!' he declared, sitting on the bed to watch them. Soon he realised the toys weren't behaving. Each time he wriggled, they wriggled too.

'Mummy lies down next to me to help me sleep,' he remembered. 'I'll lie down next to you so that you can take your nap.'

Soon little Roo was fast asleep too, dreaming of sticks, houses and bouncing games…

It was late in the afternoon when Roo woke from his nap. He bounced out of bed and into the kitchen. Kanga had prepared a delicious snack for him – a glass of juice, some bread with mustard and a hot bowl of soup.

'This will give you lots of energy for all that fun you're going to have,' smiled Kanga.

'Yummy!' Roo exclaimed happily.

As soon as he had finished, Roo dashed outside to meet his friends.

Everyone had finished work by the
time Roo found them. Eeyore's
house was as good as new again.

'Now we can play!' shouted Roo.
Rabbit had an idea. 'Let's have a
sack race!'

Everyone scrambled about,
climbing into big canvas sacks.
Piglet and Roo shared one,
and Pooh and Tigger were
in another, with Eeyore
following behind on his own.
'Let's race!' cried Roo.
'Ready... Set... GO!' Owl
yelled, and everyone jumped
forward as fast as they
could go.

'We're winning! We're winning!' cried Roo, as he and Piglet jumped over the finishing line.

'My stomach feels all bouncy,' whined Piglet. 'It hurts!' He clutched his wobbly tummy.

'Bouncing's difficult when you've got a sack around you,' protested Tigger, out of breath. 'It's makin' me so very tired.'

'That was fun!' giggled Roo, 'Come on, let's do it again!'

But everyone except Roo had collapsed into a pile on the ground. They were much too tired to start another race.

Roo smiled. 'Sleeping in the day isn't so silly after all,' he said. 'Next time we should all take a nap!'

But his friends were sound asleep already...